MIRIAM

Book 1

A CHILD'S BIBLE KIDS

Katheryn Maddox Haddad

Northern Lights Publishing House

Cover design by Sharon Lavy &
Jim Pagett, Images licensed by Sweet
Publishing http://sweetpublishing.com

ISBN-978-1-948462-00-6

Printed in the United States.

NOTE: The author used one-syllable words as much as
possible. Longer words were sometimes hyphenated to help
the child pronounce them.

Other Books By this Author For All Ages

HISTORICAL NOVELS
Series of 8: They Met Jesus
Ongoing Series of 8: Intrepid Men of God
Mysteries of the Empire with Klaudius & Hektor
Christmas: They Rocked the Cradle that Rocked the World
Series of 8: A Child's Life of Christ
Series of 10: A Child's Bible Heroes
Series of 8: A Child's Bible Kids
Series of 10: A Child's Bible Ladies

HISTORICAL RESEARCH BIBLE
for Novel, Screenwriter, Documentary & Thesis Writers

TOPICAL
Applied Christianity: Handbook 500 Good Works
Christianity or Islam? The Contrast
The Holy Spirit: 592 Verses Examined-
The Road to Heaven
Inside the Hearts of Bible Women-Reader+Audio+Leader
Revelation: A Love Letter From God
Worship Changes Since 1st Century + Worship 1sr Century Way
Was Jesus God? (Why Evil)
365 Life-Changing Scriptures Day by Date
The Road to Heaven
The Lord's Supper: 52 Readings with Prayers

FUN BOOKS
Bible Puzzles, Bible Song Book, Bible Numbers

TOUCHING GOD SERIES
365 Golden Bible Thoughts: God's Heart to Yours
365 Pearls of Wisdom: God's Soul to Yours
365 Silver-Winged Prayers: Your Spirit to God's

SURVEY SERIES: EASY BIBLE WORKBOOKS
→Old Testament & New Testament Surveys
→Questions You Have Asked-Part I & II

Genealogy: How to Climb Your Family Tree Without Falling Out
Volume I & 2: Beginner-Intermediate & Colonial-Medieval

Table of Contents

1 ~ Big Sister

Miriam, 3 years old, turned in circles on the sandy street in front of her family's home.

"I've got a baby! I've got a baby!" she said in her best sing-song voice.

"Don't either," the neigh-bor boy chimed in. "You're just a little girl. Little girls don't have babies. Only big girls do."

Miriam stopped swinging around and put her hands on her hips. "I'm a big girl."

"Are not," the boy said.

"My daddy said I'm a big girl."

"Are not. I'm 6 and I know those things."

"Well, I'm free years old and I'm smart."

"There you are," a big daddy voice said.

Miriam, with her black curls and rosy little-girl cheeks, looked in the direction of the voice, grinned, and held up her arms.

"You shouldn't be out in the street by yourself," Amram said as he swept her up in his big strong arms.

"Daddy," Miriam cooed, "he said I'm not big enough to have a baby, but I am, aren't I, Daddy?"

"Who told you that? Our whole family has a baby now."

Miriam, grinned big, looked around, and the neigh-bor boy was gone.

Amram took his daugh-ter back into the home his family had owned since the good times long ago when Israel-ites were loved in Egypt.

"Oh, do you hear that wailing?" He said as he set Miriam back on her own two feet.

Her eyes got big and she spoke in a growly big-girl voice. "Yeah. That's our baby Aaron, and he's mad."

"Well, we shall have to fix that," Yach-Abed called out from a nearby room above the tiny baby wail.

Miriam skipped into her mother's room and stopped next to her bed. She grinned as she looked down at the family's new little person who was still doing his best to wail with his tiny voice.

"I think your baby brother needs you to hold him and kiss him on both cheeks."

"He needs me, Mama?" Miriam asked.

"Oh, indeed, he does. Now sit on the cushion here and I will hand little Aaron down to you."

Miriam obeyed. Her grin was now gone and she got a serious look on her face.

When the new baby was settled in Miriam's lap, she promptly kissed him on both cheeks. She brushed his wispy silky black hair away from his forehead and sang. As she did, baby Aaron looked up into her eyes and stopped crying.

After a while, she stopped singing because baby Aaron was now fast asleep.

"Mommy," Miriam whispered, looking up at her mother. "Can I always take care of him?"

"Oh, I am de-pend-ing on it. You are a good big sister. When he gets older, you can even play with him."

"Even when he's as big as Daddy?" Miriam asked.

"Maybe," Yach-Abed replied with a grin. "If he isn't taking care of you by then."

THINK & DO

1.   Do you have a younger brother or sister? Are you sometimes mad that it takes more time for your parents to take care of it than it does to take care of you? Why do you think that is?

2.   In what ways can you help take care of your younger brother or sister so your parents will have more time for you?

2 ~ Slaves

Miriam is now 4 years old.

"Now, Sweetie," Yach-Abed said. "When you go to work with me, I need you to keep close watch over Aaron. He does not under-stand he cannot play close to the river where the big crock-o-diles are."

"Yeah," Mariam replied. "They have big mouths and teeth and would eat him all up."

"And he cannot play close to piles of bricks. Do you re-mem-ber why?" her mother asked.

"Yes. Because there are snakes under them that would bite him."

"That's right. Now climb up into the cart so Daddy can take us to work."

The sun was not up yet, but Miriam's family joined the other families in Goshen as they made their two-hour walk to Ramses, the new city the slaves were being forced to build.

"But, Mommy, why do you have to go to work every day? Why can't you stay home and bake and sew things and just Daddy go to work?"

"Well, we Israel-ites are forced to work. We do not have a choice."

"Why?"

"It's the law that Pha-raoh made."

"And they will put Daddy in jail if we don't go?" Miriam asked.

The ques-tion was not answered. Miriam heard her mother sniff and knew she was crying. She was sorry she asked her quest-ion.

She watched her father as he

pulled the cart with his family on it. She felt lucky they even had a cart. Some little children had to be carried by their parents to their place of work.

She barely re-mem-bered when the family donkey had died. Her father had just said, "The Lord gives and the Lord takes away. Blessed be the name of the Lord." Miriam had often wondered what that meant.

The family was quiet until they reached the new city with bricks everywhere to make walls and buildings with.

Amram set the cart down and walked around to his family. He helped his wife, his little girl Miriam, and his little boy Aaron down off the cart.

He kept 1-year-old Aaron in his big strong arms a little longer. "Now you obey your big sister, Aaron. She loves you. And stay away from the river."

"Okey, dokey," Aaron said as his father kissed him on both cheeks, then set him down on his own two feet.

Miriam's mother and father hugged and parted to begin their work.

"Now you and Aaron go over there and play while I pick up straw to make the bricks," Yach-Abed said.

"Aaron, you can't catch me," big girl

Miriam called out to her brother. As she pretended to run from him, he giggled and toddled after his big sister.

After a long time, they heard a bell. Yach-Abed walked over.

"Did you pack the bread and cucumbers for our lunch? We all depend on you to do that."

THINK & DO

1.   Back in Bible times, a lot of people were made slaves if they lived in a land belonging to someone else. Being a slave means you have to work but are never paid. You have to do whatever your master tells you to.

As a child, you are not old enough to be paid to do chores for the family. Would you be happier if you got down on the floor and kicked and screamed because you were not paid? Or would you be happier if you smiled and did your chores anyway? Which way would you smile more?

2.   Miriam, being the oldest of the children, had more chores to do than

Aaron. Why was that? Do you think she got to do more play things than Aaron too?

In your family, what chores does the oldest child have to do? What play things does the oldest child get to do the younger children cannot yet?

3 ~ All the Boy Babies

"No!" big, strong Amram bell-owed, pacing back and forth across the court-yard of the family's long-time home.

"No!" he bellowed again. "I will not allow it."

Miriam, now 5 years old, always became scared when her father got like this. She knew he was not mad at her, but it scared her anyway.

She looked over at her mother. Yach-Abed was crying. Aaron was tugging at her skirt for her to pick him up.

Miriam ran over and took Aaron's chubby hand and led him to a corner where they could roll a ball between their legs to each other.

She watched her father step over to her seated mother and kneel down before her. He gently helped her stand and the two leaned on each other. She thought she even saw a tear in her father's eye.

"They cannot do that to us," Yach-Abed said between sobs. "How much more can we take?"

"Shhh, my love," Amram said. "Surely the God of our great-great-grandfathers—Abraham, Isaac, and Jacob—will rescue us from this slavery someday."

"And all the horrid things they are doing to us," Yach-Abed added as she wiped her eyes with the edge of her sleeve.

Miriam waited until her parents sat down on a bench together. Her father's strong arm wrapped around her delicate mother. They became quiet.

"Mommy," Miriam finally had the nerve to say, "Why is Daddy mad and why are you crying?" She was almost afraid to know the answer.

"It's a good thing Aaron was born when he was," Amram mumbled. "But where is the God of Abraham, Isaac, and Jacob now to help us?"

"Mommy, what's wrong? Why is it a good thing Aaron was born when I was 3 years old?"

"I heard Pha-raoh ordered the midwives who helped babies be born to do it. But they wouldn't," Amram added.

"Do what, Daddy? Why are you so mad? Why is Mommy crying?" Miriam asked again.

Her parents did not answer. Miriam

resumed playing with her little brother, now 2 years old.

"No!" Amram said finally, standing and walking back and forth again. "I forbid it."

"Daddy?" Miriam asked. "What do you forbid?"

"Sweetheart," Yach-Abed said, standing and stepping over to her husband. "You cannot forbid it. The Egypt-ians rule the country; We don't. You know that."

Once more, Miriam's parents embraced.

"Mommy! Daddy! You're scaring

me," Miriam said, leaving Aaron to play with the ball alone and walking over to her parents.

Amram stooped and looked into the eyes of his daugh-ter. "Your mother is going to have another baby."

Miriam was con-fused. "But I thought that is a happy thing. I can have another little brother or sister."

"Sweetie," Yach-Abed said, "The Egypt-ians are afraid of us. There are more Israel-ites than Egypt-ians. From now on... From now on... From now on, they are going to throw all boy babies in the river."

THINK & DO

1.   Sometimes sad things happen in families. That is when it is important for brothers and sisters, mommies and daddies, grandpas and grandmas to help each other and just be sad together for a while.

Has your family gone through a sad thing? What was it? Draw a picture for someone in your family who is crying about it. Tell them you love them.

If not, perhaps the person reading to you or someone else knows a family going through something sad. Find out who it is and draw them a picture telling them that you love them.

2.   Always re-mem-ber that, if a little child dies, they get to be with Jesus and be happier than ever.

4 – Trading Places

Days and weeks and months went by. Every morning way before daylight, the family went out to the cart, climbed in, and Amram, with his big muscles, pulled his family to Ramses, the city Egypt's slaves were building.

As always, Yach-Abed worked at picking up straw for the brick makers. The straw helped hold the clay together and make strong bricks for strong walls.

"Miriam," Amram said one morning when they arrived at their work place. "Your mommy's tummy is getting so big, it is getting in her way. When she bends over to pick up the straw, she can hardly find it."

"Oh, Daddy," 6-year-old Miriam said, smiling. "I know what you're going to say. You want me to trade places with Mommy so she can play with Aaron and I can pick up straw."

"You are such a smart little girl," Amram said, grinning.

Miriam put her hands on her hips. "I am not a little girl."

"Oh, pardon me," her father said.

"You are a smart big girl."

As her father winked at her and took little Aaron in his strong arms, Miriam walked over to where her mother was trying to pick up straw and took her place.

After that, Yach-Abed gathered several children around her and played games with them.

"Why does Mommy play with so many children, Daddy? Why doesn't she just play with Aaron?"

"She does not want our masters to know she is going to have a baby. If they know, they will watch our house and, as soon as the baby is born, grab it from us."

"Oh," Miriam said. "Mommy is pretending she has a new job."

"Well, it is a new job," Amram said. "She is helping other mothers so they can work harder. Our masters like that."

Late one afternoon, Aaron toddled over to Miriam as she picked up straw. He tugged at her sleeve. "Mommy crying, Mir," he said.

"Go back over there," Miriam warned. "Mommy cries a lot."

"Mommy hurting. Mommy hurting."

Miriam looked over at her mother who was lying flat on her back on the ground. She knew.

"Hurry! Go back to Mommy and giggle a lot. Pretend you and Mommy are playing a game. Okay, Aaron?"

"Okay, Mir," he said.

Miriam took off running into the city of Ramses. "God of Abraham, Isaac, and that last one," she prayed as she ran, "help me find my daddy."

She ran up and down the streets of the new city looking for her father. She looked down and she looked up.

She spotted him on a roof pulling

bricks up by a rope.

"Daddy! Daddy!" she called up.

Amram spotted his daugh-ter and quickly climbed down to her. "Hurry and tell me while my master is not looking. What is happening? Is it your mother?"

"She is hurting, just like you told me she would."

"And did you tell Aaron to pretend he is playing a game with her like I told you to do?"

THINK & DO

1. Did you ever have to trade places with someone who couldn't do their work? Maybe it was a brother or sister. Maybe it was a neigh-bor or a friend at school. Tell about it.

2. Do you know anyone who is sick and needs you to help them at their house? Maybe you can sweep their floor or serve a drink to them. Ask the person reading to you or anyone in your house if they know someone you can help. When you are done with this chapter, make arrange-ments to help that person.

5 ~ Fooled

"Hurry! Run back to your mother," Amram told Miriam.

As she walked away, she could hear her father say something very loud to his master. She knew the master had a whip and could beat her father, so prayed to the God of Abraham, Isaac and the third one she could never re-mem-ber to be with her father.

Then she heard yelling. Her father

was yelling, then his master was yelling.

"Take that and that and that," her father's master shouted. She re-cog-nized the snap of the whip. Even worse, she re-cog-nized the cries of her father.

Miriam ran as hard and as fast as she could to her mother. When she arrived, Aaron was sitting next to their mother looking con-fused. Miriam made herself laugh. Amid her tears she laughed and laughed and laughed.

"Oh, this is a fun game, Mommy," Miriam said as loud as she could so the masters watching them would not realize her mother was about to have a baby. Every time her mother began to call out in pain, Miriam laughed. The louder her mother cried out, the louder Miriam laughed. "Ha, ha, ha," she said even though she was crying.

"Is she okay?" It was the voice of Amram.

Miriam turned to see her father bent over and bleeding. "Daddy. What did they do to you?"

"Oh, Miriam, it was just a game. I let him beat me so I could have an excuse to go home." He forced a smile. "It worked. I get to take your mother home now."

Amram waited until the master over the brick makers was not looking, picked up his wife, and carried her to the cart.

Miriam grabbed Aaron's chubby hand and hurried him to the cart also.

"Duck down, everyone," their father said after laying his wife in the back. "I don't want them to see my family is with me."

Even though his back was hurting because of the whipping, Miriam's father grabbed the handles of the cart and pulled it out through the un-finished gate from the new city and down the road back toward their home in Goshen.

Brave Amram ran as fast as he

could until they were out in the desert away from any cities. He stopped to get his breath and ease the pain in his back, then walked around to his family.

"Sweetheart," he said to Yach-Abed, pretending his own back was not hurting, "how are you doing?"

He took one look at her and knew. "Children, go over to that bush and play for a while. I think your mother has a wonderful surprise for you."

"A present?" Aaron asked.

"Yes, a very special present," Amram replied.

Miriam took Aaron over to the bush

and played a game of counting the number of birds that flew over their head. They counted until Aaron's eyes got heavy and he fell asleep with his head on Miriam's lap.

Miriam looked down on him as she had the day he was born, brushed the hair off his forehead, kissed him on both cheeks, and sang a song until she, too, fell asleep.

"Ha! Ha!"

Miriam opened her eyes at the sound of her father's voice.

"I knew it!" he shouted. "A baby boy!"

THINK & DO

1. Has an older brother or sister ever taken the blame for something you did so they would be punished instead of you? Or perhaps you have done this for someone younger and weaker than you.

That is a very brave thing to do. When an older and stronger person takes the punishment, s/he becomes a hero.

If you know of this happening, draw a picture with the word "You are my hero" on it and give it to the older and stronger person who took the blame for someone else.

2. Have you ever done work that a

younger and weaker person was supposed
to do but couldn't? That, too, made
you a hero.

6 ~ The Basket

By the time Miriam's family got back home, it had just turned dark. They were glad. The other slaves would just now be starting home from the city they were building. That meant no one in the neigh-bor-hood was around to see them bring Miriam's new baby brother into their house.

"Would you like to see your baby brother now?" Yach-Abed asked as she sat on her usual bench in the courtyard.

6-year-old Miriam took Aaron's chubby hand and walked toward their mother, their eyes sparkling.

Yach-Abed pulled back Amram's cloak she had wrapped the baby in.

"He's red," Aaron mumbled.

"You were just as red when you were born," Miriam spouted with a grin. "Why don't you lean over and kiss him on both cheeks like I did you when you were born?"

Little Aaron obeyed.

Amram walked toward his wife leaning over with his hurt back and sat next to her. "Sweetheart," he said, "let me take him and you try to sleep."

Yach-Abed handed the baby over to her husband. "Yes, I will need to return to work tomorrow. They cannot know... They cannot know..."

"We will think of some way to keep him hidden," he assured her. "Miriam will stay home with the baby. They will not find our son. I forbid it."

Every morning before daylight, Amram pulled the cart with Yach-Abed and Aaron in it all the way to the city of Ramses the slaves were building.

"So far, they have not ques-tioned Miriam staying home," Yach-Abed said each day. "I wonder how long it will last."

"Well, while the baby sleeps, she has been able to weave enough cloth for us to have clothes as soon as these wear out. It is not done very well but is good enough for slaves," Amram said.

"Yes, her cloth is strange looking. But, for a 6-year-old, she has done very well," Yach-Abed said.

"We will keep praying to the God of Abraham, Isaac, and Jacob," Amram said.

5 weeks went by. 8 weeks. 10 weeks.

One night after they arrived home,

there was a loud banging on their gate.

As soon as they heard it, Miriam now 7 years old, grabbed the baby. She ran up onto the roof of their house, and down a ladder they had placed at the back in case they had to escape.

"We know you're in there!" the gruff voice shouted. "Open up!"

Amram walked slowly to the gate and opened it.

"You said that daugh-ter of yours had to stay home and weave cloth to replace those holey things you are wearing," the soldier said. "Well, she has had more than enough time. Where is she?"

"I'm right here," Miriam said from on top of their flat roof.

"She will report to work tomorrow morning or you will be given 100 lashes," the soldier shouted at Amram.

With that, he turned back out onto the street, climbed onto his horse, and galloped away.

"Where is my baby?" Yach-Abed called up to Miriam?

"He's at the bottom of the ladder fast asleep. I will get him now," she said already turning toward the back of their old house.

Amram took a deep breath and pulled on his beard. "We cannot take any chances. You cannot take the baby to work. He is too big for you to hide, and his voice is getting stronger."

Yach-Abed sighed, walked over to a room where they kept supplies, and brought out a half-made basket.

"Now is not the time to be weaving baskets," Amram said.

"This is not just any basket," she said, looking over at her husband. Tears came to her eyes. "Just as a boat on the waters saved Noah and his family, this tiny boat on the waters of our Nile River will save our baby."

No one said anything. They stared at the basket. They stared at the baby now wiggling in Miriam's unsteady arms. They stared at the trembling lips and misting eyes of Yach-Abed.

"I will work on the basket the rest of the night," she said.

"It is the only way, isn't it?" Amram groaned.

"Yes. It is the only way to save our baby," she whispered.

THINK & DO

1.   Sometimes we are sad for a very long time before we can smile again. It can happen when someone is sick a long time, then finally gets well.

Do you know someone who was sick a long time and now is well and smiling again? Draw a picture with a sun in the middle. Write on it, "God helped you get well. God made you happy again."

If you cannot write, draw a picture of the person in a bed on the front of your paper and a picture of the person standing up and smiling on the other side of the picture.

When you give that person your picture, smile and tell them God made them well and happy again.

7 ~ The River

It was now dark out. Amram picked up the basket. He looked at the top and the bottom. He looked at each side. He looked at the front and the back.

"We do not have time for you to weave any more on the basket," he said in almost a whisper. "That gum acadia tree growing behind our house will provide the resin we will need to line the basket and keep the water out. If

I go out now and put the resin all over the basket, it will hopefully be dry by morning. If it is not, it will still work, and the resin will not hurt our baby." Then he left.

With tears, Yach-Abed took her baby from Miriam and held it close to her. She walked and walked with it, singing and talking to it.

"I will never forget you, my little baby son. You will forget me, but you will always be in my heart."

She was still walking and talking and singing when her husband returned with the resin from the tree. He put the resin in a bowl.

"Miriam, come hold the bowl for me," her father said.

Miriam held the bowl of acacia resin while her father dipped his hands in it and smeared it all over the basket. There wasn't enough.

Amram rushed back outside and behind the house. He stayed longer this time. When he came back the bowl was full of resin again. "I had to find another tree in the dark," he said. His eyes were swelled. Miriam knew her father had been crying while he was behind their house.

Once again, Miriam held the bowl while her father smeared its contents on the basket to make it water tight.

At last he stood. He took the basket and hung it from a large peg in the wall.

That night, no one slept except Aaron. And sometimes Miriam.

"Wake up," she heard. It was her mother. "It is time," she whispered.

The sun not up quite yet. "Did you not go to work, Mamma? The slave masters will be angry."

"Let them be angry," Yach-Abed said.

"We are ready. After I set the basket and our baby in the river, you are to follow it until it stops. Your father and Aaron and I will go on to work then. And we will pray all day."

Amram opened the gate. Together, the family went out of the gate and walked in the shadows down to the Nile River.

"You will never let the basket and your baby brother out of your sight until it can go no farther," Amram said with a raspy voice.

"Then you will report back to us what happened," Yach-Abed said with a trembling voice.

"We never named him," Miriam said as they slowly walked toward the river. "Who will we pray for?"

"God knows who he is," Yach-Abed said as she kneeled by the river. Then, trying to control her tears, she kissed her baby boy on both cheeks, set him in the basket on the water, and watched him float away.

"Go!" Amram said, his manly voice trembling. "Go. Never lose sight of him. Go."

As the sun came up, Miriam knew her parents and Aaron would be making their way to the city of Ramses being built by the slaves—being built by her mother and father. And she knew, every step they took, would be a prayer for their baby boy who they never named.

Sometimes the basket stopped among the bul-rushes and Miriam was afraid a crock-o-dile would jump out of the water and grab her baby brother. But the basket always wiggled free and go on down the river.

The baby began crying. "Oh, no! He is going to be discovered," Miriam whispered to herself. "Stop crying, baby. Oh, God, make our baby stop crying."

But the more Miriam prayed, the louder the baby cried. Pretty soon she could see his little arms and legs raised above the edge of the basket, wiggling as he cried.

She heard giggling, but it wasn't the

baby. Then more giggling. She looked in the direction of the giggles and saw a grand house up on a hill overlooking the river.

Down by the shore she saw maids. And she saw a pretty lady giving orders to her maids. "I hear a baby," she told them. "Find it. Bring it to me."

The maids waded out into the river and found the basket with Miriam's baby brother in it. Miriam gasped.

THINK & DO

1.   Sometimes people run in a race and cannot finish. Sometimes it is because they twisted their ankle. Sometimes it is because they ran out of breath. Sometimes it is just too far and they run out of energy. But they struggle in last place and cross the finish line just so they can say they didn't quit.

Life is like that too. There are some people who cannot see as well as they used to. But they don't stay home. Some people cannot walk as well as they used to. But they don't stay home. Do you know someone who is partly blind or partly lame? Tell them, "I want to be brave like you."

8 ~ The Palace

Miriam watched the pretty lady and wondered if she would hand the baby over to a soldier to throw it into the river.

She didn't. Instead, the pretty lady walked around with Miriam's baby brother swaying and singing a lullaby.

Miriam watched for a very long time from her hiding place. She watched as the pretty lady calmed her baby brother and he fell asleep. She watched and watched and watched.

After a while, he woke up and began to cry again.

"Oh, no," Miriam muttered aloud.

But the pretty lady did not frown. She smiled. "I believe our baby is hungry. Oh, my. What shall we do?"

Before Miriam knew she had done it, she jumped out of her hiding place. She pretended to wander over to the pretty lady. She overheard the maids talking to their mistress.

"Princess, shall I get a nurse for him?" a maid asked.

Miriam kept pretending to just wander over in their direction. "Oh, where am I?" she asked as the princess and her maids looked over at her.

"Oh, look at the baby. Can I hold him?" Miriam said.

"Who are you? Are you one of the slave girls?" the Princess said. "You must leave. You are all dirty. Have you been playing in the river? You smell like seaweed."

"The baby had stopped crying for a moment, then started again.

"Is he hungry?" Miriam asked, hoping she was not saying the wrong thing. "My mommy is a nurse. Would you like to have a nurse for your baby?"

The princess stared at Miriam. Miriam stared at the princess. The princess smiled.

"That will be fine. When can she be here to feed the baby?"

"I don't know, but maybe soon," Miriam said, realizing her mother was far away at work. "I will run now and find her."

Miriam ran toward home, not knowing what to do. When she got there, she started to climb over the front gate because her father had the only key to the lock and he and her mother were both at work.

As the gate rattled, she heard voices. She jumped back down just as she heard her mother's voice.

"Who is it?" her mother said just loud enough she could be heard. "Whoever you are, it is too late. I have no baby boy."

"Mommy?" Miriam said through the gate.

The gate opened and Miriam rushed into her mother's arms.

"You're home! You didn't go to the big bad city where our masters are so mean. They will beat Daddy."

"Your father said he would tell them I was sick, for that I am. I cannot eat, I cannot think. My heart is so lonely for your baby brother." Her eyes were swelled and her voice trembly.

"Mommy. Mommy," Miriam said, re-mem-bering her mission. "He is safe!"

"He is?"

"Yes, he floated to a big house and a princess got him."

"A princess?"

"Yes, and he is crying and hungry, and I told her you were a nurse and..."

"You showed yourself to the princess?"

Miriam stopped and realized what she had done. "Oh. I guess I did."

"And she didn't beat you?"

"No. She said I smelled like sea weed, but when I told her you could feed the baby, she told me to get you. I didn't know what I was going to do because I thought you had gone to that city you and Daddy are building, and...."

"Slow down, my child," Yach-Abed said, smiling for the first time in a long time. "She wants me to nurse our baby? Oh, praise be the God of Abraham, Isaac and Jacob."

Miriam took her mother's hand and tugged on it. "Come fast, Mommy. She wants you fast."

So, Miriam led her mother a long way until they came to the big house. The princess was gone, but one maid was still down by the water.

"Is this your mother, the nurse?" the maid asked as Miriam and her mother came close.

"Yes. My mother is ready to be a nurse to the baby."

"Follow me," the maid said.

THINK & DO

1.   Do you know anyone who has a new baby? Draw a picture of a baby and a heart to give to the parents.

If you do not know anyone with a new baby, perhaps your newspaper will have baby announce-ments in it. Have a grownup look in a tele-phone book to see if s/he can find an address to send your picture of a baby to.

9 ~ Moses

Soon, the word was all over Egypt. "The princess, Pha-raoh's daugh-ter, has adopted a baby. She named him Moses."

"That's an odd name for a baby," many said. "It means brought out of water."

"That's what happened. She found her baby in the water."

Years passed. Miriam's mother nursed baby Moses. Then, when he got a little older, the princess let Yach-Abed stay on as his nurse to teach him how to walk. Then she taught him how to read and write the language of her people, the Israel-ites.

"You must never tell anyone you know this lan-guage," Yach-Abed would warn Moses after every lesson.

More years passed. Miriam was 16, then 26, then 36, then 46. Miriam, of course, went to the city of Ramses which they were still building to pick up straw with her mother.

Little brother, Aaron, of course,

was now 43 and much bigger than his older sister.

Moses' mother and father, his big sister, Miriam, and his big brother, Aaron, were careful not to call out to him whenever Moses rode his chariot through the city, inspecting it. They didn't whenever soldiers marched by with Prince Moses leading them either. They needed to help protect Moses. Everyone thought he was Egypt-ian and not a Jew.

One day there was loud shouting coming from a part of the city where a special building was being built. Miriam looked up just in time to see her brother, Prince Moses, in his chariot, racing toward the palace.

"Stop him!" she heard someone else say. "He killed an Egypt-ian. Now he is going to kill us."

Miriam was shocked. Things settled back down the rest of the day. When it began to be dark and the slaves quit their work, she was joined by her mother. They waited by the same old cart they had used since Miriam was a little girl.

After a while old Amram and Aaron arrived at the cart. Amram and Yach-Abed climbed on board. Aaron picked up the bars that used to be attached to a donkey Miriam didn't re-mem-ber, and began walking toward their home in Goshen. Miriam walked beside brother

Aaron so as to not add to the weight to the cart.

"What happened?" she asked him as they walked. "Was Moses involved?"

"It was bad," Aaron replied. "Real bad. Moses was out here yesterday trying to defend our people and acci—dent-ally killed one of our Egypt-ian masters. He came back today and tried to break up a fight between two slaves."

"Well, why would he run from that?"

"Word had already spread that he had killed our Egypt-ian master. He was the head master over all the

others. He was related to Pha-raoh
somehow."

"Oh, no. If they catch Moses…"

Miriam and Aaron said no more the
rest of the way home. When they
arrived and all went inside for the
night, Amram stood before the family.

"We shall pray mightily for our son
and your brother. The God of
Abraham, Isaac and Jacob saved him
once before. He will save him again."

Miriam and her family never heard
from Moses again. Was he dead or
alive?

THINK AND DO

1. Did you ever try to help someone and everything turned out worse than what it was? Perhaps you were helping with the dishes but one dropped and broke. Perhaps you were helping mow the lawn and the lawnmower stopped working. You thought you had only made things worse by trying to help.

The Bible says in Romans 8:28 that God can make everything turn out to some kind of good if we love him. If you can read and write, copy that verse on a piece of paper and tape it to a wall in your room or the re-frig-er-a-tor.

10 ~ Freedom

More years passed. No one ever heard from Moses again. Miriam often thought back to all the things the family went through to save his life.

"All for nothing," she was often heard to mutter under her breath.

The city of Ramses was finally completed. Now the Egypt-ians put the slaves to work in a royal cemetery where Pha-raohs were buried. They built high buildings that were triangle on all sides and called pyr-a-mids.

They had just finished building one when Pha-raoh died. Now there was a new Pha-raoh. He had been raised with Moses. Would he try to find Moses and bring him back? Or was Moses even alive any more?

Amram and Yach-Abed had died a few years earlier and were buried in the sands of Egypt.

"Miriam, I had a dream last night," Aaron told his sister one day while pulling a basket out of their store room. "He is still alive."

"Who is still alive?"

"Moses," he said, putting some cheese and dates in the basket. "God spoke to me in my dream. Moses is on his way back here. God told him it was time to free us."

Miriam stared at her brother. "What are you doing?"

"I'm packing," Aaron said. "God told me Moses is afraid to come back. I am supposed to give him cour-age and tell him what the Pha-raoh he grew up with is like. I am supposed to be Moses' spokesman."

"To Pha-raoh? He will have you both killed," Miriam warned.

"God said he will not be able to touch us. He has given so much power to Moses, the Egypt-ians will beg us to leave."

"No one has that much power," Miriam said. "We have been here 430 years since Joseph brought our families here and we have been slaves for 400 of those years. Egypt will never let us go."

Aaron said no more. He brushed the hair off his sister's forehead, kissed her on both cheeks, and left. "Will I ever see you again?" she called after him. "Or will I be left with no brothers at all?"

Miriam waited at home 1 week, then

2, then 3. One evening, there was a knock on her gate. Was it soldiers? Had they caught both of her brothers and now were after her?

She took a deep breath and opened the gate. There stood Aaron. And guess what. There stood Moses too!

Miriam grinned. Her brothers grinned. Then they laughed and cried at the same time.

Moses stepped forward and grabbed his older sister who he now towered over, hugged her, and swung her in a circle in the middle of the courtyard. They were so happy to see each other after 40 long years.

Many things happened after that. Moses and Aaron marched into the palace without anyone stopping them. Pha-raoh yelled at them, and Moses and Aaron yelled back.

"God said these slaves are his people and you are to set them free."

"No. Never," Pha-raoh would always yell.

One by one, Moses held his shepherd's staff up in the air and a different terrible thing would happen to Egypt. Once he turned the Nile River to blood and yelled, "God said these slaves are his people and you are to set them free."

"Okay," Pha-raoh said long enough to turn the river back into water. He lied. The slaves were stuck in Egypt.

Another time Moses sent hail down from the sky and it ruined the crops so people couldn't eat.

"Okay," Pha-raoh said long enough for Moses to make the hail to stop. He always lied. The slaves were stuck in Egypt.

Another time Moses ordered millions of grass-hoppers to come eat up even the stalks of the crops. Now there was nothing even for animals to eat so they could live.

"Okay," Pha-raoh said long enough

for for Moses to send the grass-
hoppers away. He always lied. The
slaves were stuck in Egypt.

But Moses was stubborn. Aaron
was stubborn. God was stubborn. With
no crops left, hardly any animals left,
and everyone crying, Pha-raoh said yes.

At long last, after a life of being a
slave, Miriam walked beside her
brothers as they led the Israel-ite
slaves out of Egypt and to freedom.

Three nights later when everyone
was safe on the other side of a great
sea, the brothers and their sister sat
around a campfire. Miriam reached up
and brushed the hair off Moses'
forehead and kissed him on both

cheeks.

"I am so proud of you, Moses," she said. "God is too."

THINK & DO

1. It took Moses a long time to do what he wanted to do—free his people of their slavery. He was 80 years old by the time he was able to do it.

Is there something you dream of doing that is very important? Is it something that will help other people? Write it down on a piece of paper. Draw a picture of you doing that thing. Put it in a special place where you can save it until you are all grown up. Never forget your dream. Always pray about your dream. If it is a good dream, God will help you accom-plish it someday. Maybe it won't be in the way you think. Maybe it will be in a special way that you haven't even thought of yet.

Thank You

Thanks for reading my book! I'm so honored that you chose to spend your precious time with my characters and entrusted me to your child. You are appreciated.

I'm an independent author who relies on my readers to help spread the word about stories you enjoy. Would you take a few minutes to let your friends know on Facebook, Pinterest... wherever you hang out online?

Also, each honest review at online retailers means a lot to me and helps other readers know if this is a book they might enjoy.

I welcome contact from readers. At my website (below), you can do so. You can also sign up for my monthly newsletter (below) to be notified of new releases, half-price print books, and 99c ebooks.

Buy Your Next Child's Book Now

Check out what they are about and get an international buy link.

A CHILD'S LIFE OF CHRIST Series of 8
http://bit.ly/ChildsLifeOfChristSet

A CHILD'S BIBLE HEROES Series of 10 books
http://bit.ly/ChildBibleHeroes

A CHILD'S BIBLE KIDS Series of 8 books
http://bit.ly/bible-kids

A CHILD'S BIBLE LADIES series of 10 books
http://bit.ly/2qmtwaA

OLD OLD STORY SET TO OLD OLD TUNES
http://bit.ly/BibleSongBook

FUN WITH BIBLE NUMBERS: 525 Problems
http://bit.ly/FunBibleNumbers

BIBLE PUZZLES FOR YOUNG & OLD
http://bit.ly/BiblePuzzlesYoungOld

About the Author

When the author was 17 some 60 years ago, she began writing her series of eight books called They Met Jesus. When she was 60, she completed it. It is now in child's form as A CHILD'S LIFE OF CHRIST.

Her four different series of children's books are most popular among grandparents and homeschoolers. But they are popular with children around the world. Her many novels and information books are popular with grownups.

Katheryn Maddox Haddad grew up in the north and now lives in Arizona where she doesn't have to shovel sunshine. She basks in 100-degree weather with palm trees, cacti, and a computer with most of the letters worn off.

Her newspaper column appeared for several years in newspapers in Texas and North Carolina – "Little Known Facts about the Bible."

She spends half her day writing, and the other half teaching English over the internet worldwide using the Bible as textbook. Students she has converted to Christianity are hiding all over the Middle East. "They are my heroes," she declares.

Each morning she sends out an inspirational scripture thought to over 30,000 people worldwide.

She is a member of Christian Writers of the West, American Christian Fiction Writers, Historical Novel Society, and the Phoenix Screen Writers Association.

Connect with the Author

Website: https://inspirationsbykatheryn.com

Facebook:
https://bit.ly/FacebooksKatherynMaddoxHaddad

Linkedin: http://bit.ly/KatherynLinkedin

Twitter: https://twitter.com/KatherynHaddad

Pinterest: https://www.pinterest.com/haddad1940/

Goodreads:
https://www.goodreads.com/katherynmaddoxhaddad

Get a Free Book

Sign up for Katheryn's monthly newsletter with half-price books for the whole family and insider tips on what's coming next.   http://bit.ly/katheryn

Join My Dream Team

Members get the first peek at my newest book and have fun offering me advice sometimes. I have a point system of rewards for helping me get the word out. Check it out here:

http://bit.ly/KatherynsDreamTeam